FREE
as a
FLEA

Written and Illustrated by:

JADE GLITHERO

AuthorHouse™ UK Ltd.
1663 Liberty Drive
Bloomington, IN 47403 USA
www.authorhouse.co.uk
Phone: 0800.197.4150

Published by AuthorHouse 04/08/2014

ISBN: 978-1-4969-7656-7 (sc)
ISBN: 978-1-4969-7657-4 (e)

authorHOUSE®

Noah

All the way to the Moon and Stars. . .

and back

Once upon a noodle
Just gone ten past three

There slept a cat
On a pea green mat

And behind his ear lived a flea

The ear was warm and cosy
And Flea was quite at home

Just now and again
It seemed quite tame

The world he'd like to roam

Cat had grown quite fond of Flea
Living behind his ear

'But the time has come
My tiny chum

For you to disappear'

I've seen the bright red bottle
And straight away I knew

Mrs Betts
Has been to the Vets

And bought. . .

Anti Flea Shampoo!

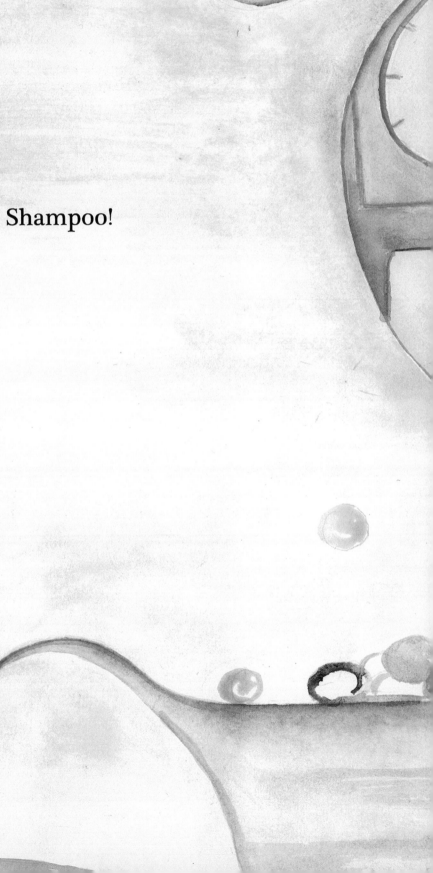
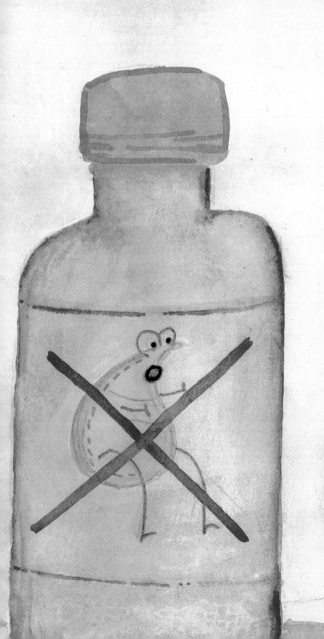
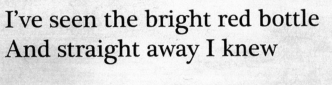

Flea Shampoo! Exclaimed the Flea
Oh deary deary me!

I'll get to the zoo
On Charlie McGoo

He's coming at half past three

Charlie McGoo was the zoo keeper
In charge of the monkey house

Perfect thought Flea
A chimpanzee

So he jumped on quiet as a mouse

'Hello' said the chimp, 'What a lovely surprise,
A friend to travel by my side'

'My name is Bungle
And I'm off to the jungle,

You can come along for the ride'

The jungle was hot and sticky
But Flea didn't like to moan

I'm free thought the flea
The world I can see

But it's not quite as comfy as home

That afternoon high in a tree
Flea met a colourful bird

A parrot called Polly
Who was ever so jolly

And this is what he heard

Tomorrow I fly to the desert
Over mountain and sea

To the edge of the sand
In a far away land

Where I'm meeting a camel for tea

Polly looked smooth and silky
Her feathers were sleek and long

She started to sing
Then stretched out her wing

And Flea with glee leapt on

The flight was long and breezy
But Flea didn't like to moan

I'm free thought the flea
The world I can see

But it's not quite as comfy as home

They arrived in the desert all sandy and hot
And there stood a glorious mammal

Flea took his chance
When they started to dance

And he leapt from parrot to camel

You speak of home so fondly
You'd like to go back I'd bet

I'm meeting a sheik
By a crystal blue lake

And he owns a jumbo jet!

The Sheik was very wealthy
His beard like a lion's mane

Flea jumped right in
And started to grin

When he saw the aeroplane

Once aboard the Sheik relaxed
And Flea began to peer

In isle number two
sat Charlie McGoo

And Flea had a Brilliant Idea!

I'll travel home on Charlie McGoo
Just like I did before

He'll get me there
In his wispy hair

I'll be home by half past four!

So . . .

Once upon a noodle
Just gone half past four

There slept a cat
On a pea green mat

When a flea sprang through the door

'I'm home! I'm home!' Exclaimed the flea
As he jumped behind Cat's ear

'Oh the places I've been!
And the things I've seen!

But there's nowhere quite like here'

CPSIA information can be obtained
at www.ICGtesting.com
Printed in the USA
LVIC04n2031050914
402719LV00006B/7